Big Dog...
Little Dog

Fred and Ted were friends.
Fred was big. Ted was little.
Fred always had money.
Ted never had money.

Beginner Books are written in simple
language especially for beginning
readers. If your child can read these
lines, then he or she will be able to
read this Beginner Book.

This book comes from
the home of
THE CAT IN THE HAT

Beginner Books
A DIVISION OF RANDOM HOUSE, INC.

*For a list of some other Beginner Books,
see the back endpaper.*

Big Dog,
Little Dog

P. D. Eastman

www.randomhouse.com/kids

Library of Congress Cataloging-in-Publication Data
Eastman, P. D. (Philip D.) Big dog . . . little dog / P. D. Eastman. p. cm. — "B-92."
SUMMARY: Two dogs are opposite in every way but are the very best of friends.
ISBN 0-375-82297-6 (trade) — ISBN 0-375-92297-0 (lib. bdg.)
[1. Dogs—Fiction. 2. Friendship—Fiction.] I. Title. PZ7.E1314 Bi 2003 [E]—dc21 2002151045

Printed in the United States of America 2003 10 9

Big Dog...
Little Dog

by P. D. Eastman

BEGINNER BOOKS®

A Division of Random House, Inc.

Fred and Ted were friends.

Fred was big.

Ted was little.

Fred always had money.

Ted never had money.

When they walked in the rain,

Fred was wet . . .

and Ted was dry.

They both liked music.

Fred played
the flute.

Ted played
the tuba.

When they had dinner,

Fred ate the spinach . . .

and Ted ate the beets.

When they painted the house,

Fred used green paint.

Ted used red.

One day Fred and Ted
went away in their cars.

Fred went in
his green car.

Ted went in
his red car.

Fred drove his car slowly.

Ted drove his car fast.

They came to a sign.

"Where should we go?" asked Fred.

"To the mountains," said Ted.

When they got to the mountains,

Ted skied all day long.

Fred skated all day long.

When they stopped,

Fred was cold.

Ted was warm.

By night both of them
were very sleepy.
"Look!" said Fred.
"A small hotel!"

Fred's room was upstairs.

Ted's room was downstairs.

"Good night, Ted.
Sleep well," said Fred.

"Good night, Fred.
Sleep well," said Ted.

But they did *not* sleep well.
Upstairs, Fred thumped and bumped
and tossed and turned.

Downstairs, Ted moaned and groaned
and crashed and thrashed all over the bed.

When morning came,
Fred called Ted.

"Let's take a walk,"
Fred said to Ted.

"We can walk
and talk," said Ted
to Fred.

They walked uphill.

They walked downhill.

They made tall talk.

They made small talk.

"My bed is too little!"

"My bed is too big!"

"What can we do about it, Ted?"

"I don't know, Fred."

"I know what to do!"
said the bird.
"Ted should sleep upstairs
and Fred should sleep
downstairs!"

"The bird's got the word."

"Back to bed!"
yelled Ted.

"Back to bed!"
yelled Fred.

"It's downstairs for me!"
yelled Fred.

"It's upstairs for me!"
yelled Ted.

Ted jumped into
the little bed upstairs.

And Fred jumped into
the big bed downstairs.

Ted slept all day long
in the cozy little bed.

And Fred slept all day long
in the cozy big bed.

"Well, that was easy to do.
Big dogs need big beds.
Little dogs need little beds.
Why make big problems
out of little problems?"

P. D. Eastman (1909–1986) was the son of an educator who was "much interested in words." That influence, combined with his work on animated films, helped make him a self-described "writer-visualizer." *Are You My Mother?* and *Go, Dog. Go!* are among the many popular books he wrote and illustrated for young readers.

Mr. Eastman's two sons followed in his creative footsteps. His eldest son, Peter Eastman (an animation artist), adds his talents to this expanded version of *Big Dog . . . Little Dog*.

Have you read
these all-time favorite
Beginner Books?

ARE YOU MY MOTHER?
by P. D. Eastman

THE BEST NEST
by P. D. Eastman

THE BIG HONEY HUNT
by Stan and Jan Berenstain

THE CAT IN THE HAT
by Dr. Seuss

FLAP YOUR WINGS
by P. D. Eastman

GO, DOG. GO!
by P. D. Eastman

MONSTER MUNCHIES
by Laura Numeroff

SAM AND THE FIREFLY
by P. D. Eastman